Earl's Big Adventure in Costa Rica

Hanna Haidar & Kimberly Newton

It was a sunny summer morning on Cape Cod, and John was in a hurry to get home. He had exciting news! As he ran up the driveway, he saw a familiar face in the window. His friend Earl was home!

Earl knew right away that something interesting was about to happen. John was so excited…and what was that package he was trying to hide? Earl wondered what it could be. He opened the door just as John was about to burst into the house.

1

"I got you some things you will need for the trip," said John. He handed Earl a small red backpack. Earl tried it on and grinned. It fit perfectly.

Next, John gave Earl a small blue book. "This is your passport," he explained. "You will need it to visit other countries." Earl opened the passport, and on the first page was his picture! Earl was so excited that he gave John a big monkey hug!

The very next day John and Earl got on a plane. They flew to San Jose, the capital city of Costa Rica. When they got to the airport, they went to the immigration desk. A man behind the desk asked for their passports. When the man handed back Earl's passport, it had a big red stamp on the first page!

They went to a bus stop and waited for their bus. As it pulled up to the stop, Earl became very confused. "John, this is a SCHOOL bus! We aren't going to school, are we? You told me we were going to the beach!"

John laughed. He explained that in some parts of Costa Rica, old school busses took people where they needed to go. Earl felt much better and they climbed on. The bus was very hot and crowded. The bus left the city and sped down a dirt road. It was very bumpy and Earl was bounced all over!

A very old couple got on the bus. "Earl," said John, "Let's get up so they can have our seats. We can stand." The old couple looked very tired. They thanked Earl and John by saying *Muchas gracias*!" "*De nada*," John replied.

"In Spanish," John explained to Earl, "*Muchas gracias* means 'thank you.' *De Nada* means 'you're welcome.'" Earl realized that he had a lot of new words to learn.

After a long time on the bus, Earl finally saw the beach up ahead. John and Earl got off in a small town named Santa Teresa. Earl couldn't believe how different it was from his beach town on Cape Cod! The whole town had only one road, and it was VERY muddy! John and Earl walked to a small restaurant named Soda Alejandro.

"In Costa Rica," John explained, "small restaurants are called *sodas*. Alejandro is the name of the man who owns the restaurant." They sat down and John explained all of the different foods on the menu.

John ordered a traditional meal called casado. It had chicken, rice, beans, and salad. Earl was hoping for a grilled cheese, his favorite meal! But he couldn't find it on the menu.

"Earl, why don't you try something different? A little more Costa Rican? You might not get this chance at home," suggested John. Earl thought about it and he decided to get a casado of his own. He was surprised to find out that he loved it! He ate every bite on his plate and was a stuffed little monkey afterwards.

The next morning Earl woke up early. He was in a hurry to get to the beach! He grabbed his towel and his sunglasses. He was ready! But John didn't think so.

"Earl, you need to put on sunscreen before we go to the beach. The sun here is very strong."

Earl hated how the sunscreen felt. It was slimy on his face and it made his fur stick together. He put it on anyways and so did John.

They walked barefoot down the muddy road. Pretty soon Earl and John were covered in mud up to their knees! Earl loved the way the mud squished between his little monkey toes.

When they got to the beach, the sand was very white and the water was the bluest water that Earl had ever seen. He and John washed off their muddy feet. John pointed out some surfers far out in the ocean. They looked like they were having so much fun in the big blue waves! Earl watched for a moment but soon something else caught his eye. Some children were building a sandcastle and Earl was much more interested in that.

"My, that's quite a castle," John said, but then he noticed that Earl looked sad. "What's wrong, Earl?"

"I wish that I could play with them," said Earl. "But I don't know what to say."

"I will tell you what to say," said John. "Can you say, *Hola, me llamo Earl, ¿puedo ayudarles?*"

"*Hola, me llamo Earl, ¿puedo ayudarles?*" repeated Earl. "What does that mean, John?"
"It means, 'Hi, my name is Earl, can I help?'" answered John.

Earl practiced saying the words three times. He and John walked over to the children. Earl was a very nervous monkey but the words came out perfectly.

"Sí!" all the children said. Earl looked at John.
"That means yes, Earl," said John. "Go and play!"

Earl happily joined the children. One boy spoke to him in English. The boy's name was Jose and he introduced all of his friends. They were learning English in school and they were happy to practice with Earl. They soon discovered that Earl was an expert sandcastle builder!

All week long, while John went surfing, Earl played at the beach with Jose and the other Costa Rican children. He also met other children from all over the world. They were all visiting Costa Rica with their families.

Jesse was from California, George and Stefani were from France, Julia was from Germany, and Emilio was from Argentina. The children spoke different languages, but Earl found that it wasn't hard for them to understand each other.

Everybody's favorite game was soccer. Much to Earl's surprise, he found out that in other countries the game was called football.

As for the children, they learned that monkeys are unstoppable soccer players!

Earl and John had a wonderful time in Costa Rica. Before long, a week had gone by. It was time for them to leave. They said good-bye to their new friends and made the long trip back to the airport. They passed the time on the bus by talking to the other passengers. Everyone was very impressed with how much Spanish Earl had learned in just one week.

When they finally came home to Cape Cod, Earl was exhausted and a little sad to be home. He missed Costa Rica and all of his new friends. He was feeling glum as he watched John getting ready to go back to work. John was a lifeguard. He was already wearing his red bathing suit and gray sweatshirt. John smiled as he walked to the door. He had one more surprise for Earl.

"Well, Earl," he said, "It was great fun traveling with you. I was wondering if you would like to come along with me on my next surf trip?"

Earl was beside himself with joy! He jumped up and down and made the sort of commotion that only an excited little monkey can make. When he calmed down he asked "Where are we going?"

"You'll just have to wait and see," said John. He walked out of the house and looked back. He waved at Earl, who was peeking out of the doorway. He knew that Earl would never believe where they were headed next!